W9-BXX-888

Dear Parent:

Congratulations! Your child is taking the first steps on an exciting journey. The destination? Independent reading!

STEP INTO READING® will help your child get there. The program offers five steps to reading success. Each step includes fun stories and colorful art. There are also Step into Reading Sticker Books, Step into Reading Math Readers, Step into Reading Phonics Readers, Step into Reading Write-In Readers, and Step into Reading Phonics Boxed Sets—a complete literacy program with something for every child.

Learning to Read, Step by Step!

Ready to Read   Preschool–Kindergarten
• big type and easy words • rhyme and rhythm • picture clues
For children who know the alphabet and are eager to begin reading.

Reading with Help   Preschool–Grade 1
• basic vocabulary • short sentences • simple stories
For children who recognize familiar words and sound out new words with help.

Reading on Your Own   Grades 1–3
• engaging characters • easy-to-follow plots • popular topics
For children who are ready to read on their own.

Reading Paragraphs   Grades 2–3
• challenging vocabulary • short paragraphs • exciting stories
For newly independent readers who read simple sentences with confidence.

Ready for Chapters   Grades 2–4
• chapters • longer paragraphs • full-color art
For children who want to take the plunge into chapter books but still like colorful pictures.

STEP INTO READING® is designed to give every child a successful reading experience. The grade levels are only guides. Children can progress through the steps at their own speed, developing confidence in their reading, no matter what their grade.

Remember, a lifetime love of reading starts with a single step!

To Mike A. and to Jon & Esther—
who fearlessly open every door—S. A.

Copyright © 2013 Disney/Pixar. All rights reserved. Published in the United States by Random House Children's Books, a division of Random House, Inc., 1745 Broadway, New York, NY 10019, and in Canada by Random House of Canada Limited, Toronto, in conjunction with Disney Enterprises, Inc.

Step into Reading, Random House, and the Random House colophon are registered trademarks of Random House, Inc.

Visit us on the Web!
StepIntoReading.com
randomhouse.com/kids

Educators and librarians, for a variety of teaching tools, visit us at RHTeachersLibrarians.com

ISBN 978-0-7364-3035-7 (trade)
ISBN 978-0-7364-8124-3 (lib. bdg.)

Printed in the United States of America
10 9 8 7 6 5 4 3 2 1

STEP INTO READING®

STEP 2

DISNEY · PIXAR

MONSTERS UNIVERSITY

SCARING LESSONS

By Susan Amerikaner

Illustrated by Fabio Laguna, Lori Tyminski,
Adrienne Brown, Jeff Jenney, Frank Anduiza, and the
Disney Storybook Artists

Random House 🏠 New York

Monsters University
is a school for monsters.
In the Scaring Program,
students learn
to scare humans.

The students

must be very scary.

Mike is a student.

Sulley is a student, too.

He looks scary.

He does not study.

Mike does not look scary.

He studies.

Mike and Sulley

do not like each other.

At the final
scare test,
Mike roars at Sulley.
Sulley roars at Mike.

Sulley breaks
the dean's scream can.
She kicks them out
of the Scaring Program!

Mike and Sulley
join the Oozma Kappas.
They enter the Scare
Games as a team.

The winners will get into the Scaring Program. The Oozma Kappa team wants to win!

The first event
is a race.
The teams run
into a dark tunnel.

Sulley runs ahead.

Mike runs to catch up.

Their team
is left behind.

Mike trains
the Oozma Kappas.
They work together.

One event
is a hiding game.
Don hides.
Oozma Kappa does well!

The last event
is a scaring game.
The team
must scare a robot.

The team
that gets the loudest
screams wins!

Mike goes last.

He scares his robot.

His robot screams
the loudest!
The Oozma Kappas win!

The team cheers.
They lift Mike
up in the air.

He is a hero!

Mike checks the robot.
Sulley made
the robot scream.
Sulley cheated!
He did not think
Mike was scary enough.

Mike will scare a human.

He wants to prove

he is scary!

Mike goes
to the human world.
He finds a cabin.
It is full of kids!

They are not scared
of Mike.
Mike is scared
of them!

Sulley finds Mike.
They need a big scream
to get home.

Sulley is scary.

Mike is smart.

They need each other!

Sulley and Mike
work together.

Mike coaches Sulley.

Sulley roars.

They scare the humans.

The humans scream.

The screams are loud!

The door opens.
Sulley and Mike
go home!

The dean is proud.
She wishes them
good luck.

Mike and Sulley
find jobs
at Monsters, Inc.!